Princess Bess
GETS DRESSED

For Lily—M. C.

To my prince of a husband, Bob—H. M.

SIMON & SCHUSTER BOOKS FOR YOUNG READERS

An imprint of Simon & Schuster Children's Publishing Division

1230 Avenue of the Americas, New York, New York 10020

Text copyright © 2009 by Margery Cuyler

Illustrations copyright © 2009 by Heather Maione

All rights reserved, including the right of reproduction in whole or in part in any form.

SIMON & SCHUSTER BOOKS FOR YOUNG READERS is a trademark of Simon & Schuster, Inc.

Book design by Lucy Ruth Cummins

The text for this book is set in Hombre.

The illustrations for this book are rendered in ink and watercolor.

Manufactured in China

2 4 6 8 10 9 7 5 3

Library of Congress Cataloging-in-Publication Data

Cuyler, Margery.

Princess Bess gets dressed / Margery Cuyler ; illustrated by

Heather Maione.—1st ed.

p. cm.

Summary: A fashionably dressed princess reveals her favorite clothes

at the end of a busy day.

ISBN-13: 978-1-4169-3833-0

ISBN-10: 1-4169-3833-8

[1. Clothing and dress—Fiction. 2. Princesses—Fiction. 3. Stories in

rhyme.] I. Maione, Heather Harms, ill. II. Title.

PZ8.3.C99Pr 2009

[E]—dc22

2007025915

Princess Bess
GETS DRESSED

Margery Cuyler ❧ Illustrated by Heather Maione

Simon & Schuster Books for Young Readers
New York   London   Toronto   Sydney

Princess Bess had loads of clothes
made with satin, snaps, and bows,
buckles, ribbons, silk, and lace,
pearly buttons sewn in place.

Buckles

As she changed her clothes all day,
Princess Bess would sometimes say,

"What I really want to wear
is a secret I can't share."

She didn't share it, since she knew
a princess has so much to do.

At eight o'clock, in velveteen,
she dined on muffins with the queen.

Next, at ten, a pink tutu
for her class with Madame Sue.

But for art she wore a frock.
She painted until twelve o'clock.

Then for luncheon with the prince,
she wore pink pantaloons of chintz.

Her afternoon was busy too.
At a joust she wore pale blue,

then changed into another dress
for her daily game of chess.

She changed again at half past three
to join the king for cake and tea.

But at six, a muslin gown,
a velvet cape, a ruby crown,
since at supper she would meet
all the guests who came to eat.

At eight o'clock, a fancy ball
to which she wore a sequined shawl.

She danced until her feet grew red
and the queen said, "Go to bed!"

No more duties, no more cares,
Princess Bess climbed up the stairs.

Closed her curtains,

locked her door,

dropped her dress upon the floor,

tossed her clothes
across her chair,

stripped down to her underwear.

"Now I'm in my favorite clothes,"
said Princess Bess on tippy toes.

She twirled and whirled, stood on her head,
then skipped and flipped into her bed.

In a rumpled, ruffled heap,
she closed her eyes and fell asleep.